# THE PRINCESS and the PETS

**ANGELA KANTER**

ILLUSTRATED BY

**MADDY M<sup>c</sup>CLELLAN**

**KINGFISHER**

BOSTON

KINGFISHER
a Houghton Mifflin Company imprint
222 Berkeley Street
Boston, Massachusetts 02116
www.houghtonmifflinbooks.com

First published in 2008
2 4 6 8 10 9 7 5 3 1

LIBRARY OF CONGRESS CATALOGING-IN-PUBLICATION DATA
has been applied for.

ISBN 978-0-7534-6212-6

Printed in China
1TR/1107/WKT/SCHOY(SCHOY)/115MA/C

# Contents

Chapter One

4

Chapter Two

13

Chapter Three

24

Chapter Four

38

Chapter Five

42

# Chapter One

"Why can't I have a pet?" Princess Mina asked the queen.

"Because they make a mess," said the queen.

"So does she," said Princess Mina, looking at her teenage sister, Princess Tina. She was slumped on the floor in the middle of a pile of magazines and half-empty mugs.

"Why can't I have a pet, Daddy?" asked
Princess Mina.
"They smell," said
the king.
"And they leave
hairs everywhere."

"So does Princess Tina!" said Princess
Mina. "She stinks!"

She turned up her nose at her sister, who
was only just visible through a haze of
perfume and hair spray. It was like an
explosion in a flower shop.

"And look—" said Princess Mina, pulling
a handful of hairs from the royal beanbag,
where Princess Tina had been sitting and
brushing her long hair.

"I'll ask Nana for a pet," said
Princess Mina. "She's a softy."
She edged over to the rocking chair
where Nana was knitting a long scarf.

"You'd like a cat or a dog, wouldn't you,
Nana?" cooed Princess Mina.

9

"Try this on, dear," said Nana, wrapping the scarf around the princess's neck ten times, until she could hardly breathe.

"It's your birthday present," Nana said cheerfully.

"But I really wanted a . . . oh, never mind,"
said Princess Mina. "It's lovely, Nana."

Princess Mina felt like crying. "I'm never going to get a pet," she said with a sigh. Then she had a brilliant idea.

# Chapter Two

"I'm going to ask my fairy godmother
for a pet," said Princess Mina.
"That's what they're for, after all—
granting wishes."
She went up to her room.

All of her dresses were hanging out of her closet and her books were all over the bed.

Her crown was lying on the table.

It was bent, as if it had been tried on by

someone whose head was much too big.

Princess Mina marched downstairs
again to see Princess Tina.
"You've been borrowing my stuff
without asking again, haven't you?"
asked Princess Mina.

"Yeah . . ." said Princess Tina. She was
stuffing her face with marshmallows.
Princess Mina's marshmallows. The ones
that Nana had given Princess Mina last
week as a reward for helping unravel
her knitting wool.

"And don't go telling Mom and Dad or that stupid fairy godmother of yours that I've used your stuff," said Princess Tina, "or I'll pull your hair so hard that you'll have to ask Nana to knit you a wig!"

"And you're never going to get a pet from anyone for your birthday, ever, because all pets make me sneeze! So there!"

*Making toads? Did she mean making toast?*
Mina wondered. Her fairy godmother
was not very good at texting and often
pressed the wrong buttons.

Princess Mina texted back. "Would like a pet for my birthday."

At once, her fairy godmother sent back a spell.

Princess Mina read it out carefully.

There was a loud bang and the castle shook.

"Oh no," said Princess Mina.
"Princess Tina's plugged in her hair
straighteners and blown a fuse again."
But it wasn't that. It was something
much more exciting.

# Chapter Three

The pets were arriving!

In the kitchen, kittens jumped out of the
blackberry pie that the king was making.

In the living room, puppies popped up
on the couch next to the queen and
chewed up her slippers as she snoozed
in front of the TV.

In the bedroom, two glistening goldfish swam around and around Nana's dentures.

And in the bathroom, Princess Tina reached for the soap and found herself holding a magnificent, shining turtle!

For a while, all that could be heard
in the palace was screaming
and shouting—with a few
meows and yelps.

Princess Mina ran from room to room,
greeting all of her wonderful new pets.

But an hour later, she
didn't feel quite so happy.

"No birthday cake unless you get rid of the pets, I'm afraid," said the king, scraping his blackberry pie into the trash.

"This pie is full of cat hair.
I'll never be able to make you
a birthday cake with all of
these kittens in the kitchen."

31

"The puppies will have to go, too," said
the queen. "My slippers will never be the
same again."

Nana tried to say
something . . .

. . . but she spat out
a goldfish instead.

Princess Tina was the angriest of them all.
The turtle had made her break out in pimples,
and when she'd gone to steal some of
Princess Mina's makeup to cover them up,
she picked up a powder puff and found that
it was a hamster.

And then she realized that maybe it hadn't been such a good idea to eat those "chocolate drops" that she'd found next to Princess Mina's bed.

"Get rid of all these pets!" she hissed to her sister.

A boa constrictor hissed back peacefully from under the bed.

Princess Mina just did
not know what to do.

# Chapter Four

"Get rid of all these pets!" said Princess
Tina in a more wobbly voice this time.
"Or—or—I'll get my fairy godmother
to turn you into a frog."

But talking about frogs reminded Princess
Tina of her dear Prince Bertram, who was
doomed to live as a little green creature
in the pond. She started to cry and
completely forgot about being
mean to Princess Mina anymore.

Princess Mina
began to feel sorry
for her sister. She
texted her fairy godmother again.

"Please send a spell
to take away the
pets," she typed.

Immediately, her fairy
godmother sent back
this message:

"A spell to take
away the pest."

Another typing mistake, Princess Mina
guessed. She read out the spell carefully.

There was another huge bang and the
castle shook again.

Was everything fixed now?

# Chapter Five

The fairy dust settled. Princess Mina looked around. The king came into the room with a handful of kittens.

"I suppose they're actually very sweet," he said. "They can stay."

The queen came running
in with the puppies at her
heels.

"They're all right," she said.

"I'm training them to
bring me my newspaper
and slippers."

Nana came in. She had found a nice
bowl for the goldfish.

"I'm going to knit a lovely goldfish-bowl
warmer to keep the goldfish warm," she said.

It looked like the spell hadn't worked.
Princess Mina waited for her big sister to
say something horrible. But Princess Tina
was nowhere to be seen.

Suddenly, Princess Mina realized what was wrong. "A spell to take away the *pest*," she remembered. "It really did take away the pest. Princess Tina was a pest. But I wonder what's happened to her."

Out in the palace grounds, an amazed Frog Prince (once known as Bertram) was happily saying hello to his delighted Frog Princess Tina . . .

# About the author and illustrator

**Angela Kanter** sits in a newspaper office all day drinking coffee and writes children's books at night, when it's really past her bedtime. She doesn't have any pets, but her two daughters dream of owning a cat or a dog—or maybe even a peacock . . .

**Maddy McClellan** lives in Brighton, England. She says, "As a child, I was always begging my parents for pets. At one point, I had a white pony, a dog, two rabbits, four guinea pigs, a hamster, and even a couple of goldfish!" At the moment, her son, Inigo, keeps her busy, but she does have a very fat black cat named Minouche.

# Strategies for Independent Readers

## Predict

Think about the cover, illustrations, and the title
of the book. What do you think this book will be about?
While you are reading think about what may
happen next and why.

## Monitor

As you read ask yourself if what you're reading makes sense.
If it doesn't, reread, look at the illustrations, or read ahead.

## Question

Ask yourself questions about important ideas
in the story such as what the characters might
do or what you might learn.

## Phonics

If there is a word that you do not know, look carefully
at the letters, sounds, and word parts that you do know.
Blend the sounds to read the word. Ask yourself if this is
a word you know. Does it make sense in the sentence?

## Summarize

Think about the characters, the setting where the
story takes place, and the problem the characters faced
in the story. Tell the important ideas in the beginning,
middle, and end of the story.

## Evaluate

Ask yourself questions like: Did you like the story?
Why or why not? How did the author make the story
come alive? How did the author make the story fun to
read? How well did you understand the story? Maybe
you can understand it better if you read it again!